TOGETHER WE CAN!

it's cool to be kind

I can help

it's fun to share

we are kind

let's play together

saying sorry makes things better

taking turns

Laughing together

be helpful

we have fun!

we care about each other

happy cupcakes

I give great hugs

I'm here for you

best friends for ever

For Andrew, my best friend forever – C.H.

To my lovely friends from JMHS,
Ledbury 1982–1987 – A.P.

First published in 2019 by Scholastic Children's Books, Euston House, 24 Eversholt Street, London NW1 1DB
a division of Scholastic Ltd · www.scholastic.co.uk

London ~ New York ~ Toronto ~ Sydney ~ Auckland ~ Mexico City ~ New Delhi ~ Hong Kong

Text copyright © 2019 Caryl Hart · Illustrations copyright © 2019 Ali Pye
The moral rights of Caryl Hart and Ali Pye have been asserted.

All rights reserved · Printed in Malaysia

ISBN HB: 978 1407 19509 4
ISBN PB: 978 1407 17739 7

1 2 3 4 5 6 7 8 9 10

Papers used by Scholastic Children's Books are made from wood grown in sustainable forests.

SCHOLASTIC

TOGETHER WE CAN!

CARYL HART

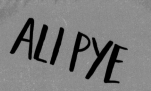

ALI PYE

A friend is a buddy, a pal or a mate,
a person who's special, who makes you feel great.

They're fun to hang out with, at home, school or play.
They're there when you need them ...

They cheer up your day!

A friend might help out
when your class work
is **tricky** ...

...or scratch your right ear
if your hands
are **all sticky!**

At school you might sit
with a new friend for lunch
and share out your snacks with a loud

munch crunch

crunch!

At playtime, a friend will take turns on the slide ...

... or count up to ten when it's your turn to hide.

Our friends are all different,
but one thing is true —

each one is quite precious, and that includes YOU!

All over the world and from since time began
we show every day that ...
TOGETHER WE CAN!

Some friends are alike,
like these two little boys —
they both have short hair
and they like the same toys.

But friends can be different and still get along.
There aren't any rules,
there is no right or wrong.

Some friends
speak a language
we don't understand.

They still laugh
together...

... and walk hand in hand.

Some people need gadgets to help them have FUN!

Whatever they use, they're great friends, every one!

Some people have one friend
and others have many.
Perhaps you know someone who doesn't have any?

If someone is lonely,
there's lots you can do.
To make them feel better, just BE a friend, too!

All over the world
and from since time began ...

... we show every day that ...

... TOGETHER WE CAN!

Some friends are nearby,
they can play every day . . .

. . . while others are distant —
they live far away.

All over the globe
there are people who care.

Just look and you'll see, there are friends everywhere.

We meet brand new people wherever we go.

Look, here are some friends who you might not yet know!

A friend can have six legs …

… or four legs …

… or two!

What kind of a friend is the best one for YOU?

All over the world
and from since time began
we show every day that ...

Pet
show

...TOGETHER WE CAN!

If YOU want a friend,
here's a thing you should know:

We MAKE friends, it's easy!
Just give it a go.

Find someone you like
and just ask them their name.

Invite them to tea, or to join in your game.

If someone is sad,
you could give them a cuddle ...

... or help them get out
of a difficult muddle!

Try baking some cupcakes,
or make a nice card.

Great
Friend
Award.

See? Making a friend
really isn't too hard.

A good friend like you
forgives any mistakes.
When you're wrong, say SORRY
with hugs or handshakes.

A nice friend like you
will be happy to share.

You'll listen and make others
feel that you care.

All over the world
and from since time began
we show every day that...

....TOGETHER WE CAN!

By making new friends we can all come together.
Be loving and kind and you'll have friends **for ever.**

smile!

feelings are important

I'll hold your hand

let's be friends

I'm good at sharing

be gentle

spread the love

hugs!

I make people laugh

there's room for you

we help each other

friends are all
around us

all join in!

a kind word can make
someone's day

we all want to be loved